♡Jamie Kiffel-Alcheh

To everyone who loves to share special traditions.
Together, we celebrate! - J.K.-A.

KAR-BEN PUBLISHING®
An imprint of Lerner Publishing Group, Inc.
241 First Avenue North
Minneapolis, MN 55401 USA
Website address: www.karben.com

Main body text set in Billy Infant Regular.
Typeface provided by SparkyType.

Library of Congress Cataloging-in-Publication Data

Names: Kiffel-Alcheh, Jamie, author. | Gallegos, Lauren, illustrator.
Title: Matzah craze / Jamie Kiffel-Alcheh, Lauren Gallegos.
Description: Minneapolis : Kar-Ben Publishing, 2021. | Audience: Ages 4-9 | Audience: Grades 2-3 | Summary: "When Noa refuses to swap anything from her lunch one day, her friends wonder why. It's because it's Passover! But friendly Noa figures out a way to bring her friends into the holiday fun"— Provided by publisher.
Identifiers: LCCN 2020013581 (print) | LCCN 2020013582 (ebook) | ISBN 9781541586680 (library binding) | ISBN 9781541586697 (paperback) | ISBN 9781728417608 (ebook)
Subjects: LCSH: Passover—Juvenile literature. | Matzos—Juvenile literature.
Classification: LCC BM695.P3 K51 2021 (print) | LCC BM695.P3 (ebook) | DDC 296.4/37—dc23

LC record available at https://lccn.loc.gov/2020013581
LC ebook record available at https://lccn.loc.gov/2020013582

Manufactured in the United States of America
1-47381-48002-5/4/2020

MATZAH CRAZE

Jamie Kiffel-Alcheh

illustrated by Lauren Gallegos

KAR-BEN
PUBLISHING

"Pop!" go boxes. "Snap!" go lids.
Lunchroom's full of hungry kids.

At Noa's school, it's time to eat.

Pizza! Pasta! Grab a seat.

"What'd you get?" friends want to know.

"How about a trade? Let's go!"

Lots of offers for a swap. . . .

Garlic bread with cheese on top?

Chicken salad spread on toast?

English muffin? Cold pot roast?

"Thanks," says Noa. "Not today.

My lunch was made a special way."

Noa's friends peek in the box.

They see cream cheese, juice, and lox,

carrot sticks, a bright green pear . . .

but what's that other thing in there?

"Might be bread," says one girl, Pat,

"but with holes—and really flat."

Noa laughs and says to her,
"This is just for Passover."

"All week long, I don't eat bread.

Matzah's what I eat instead."

"Why?" asks second-grader Pete.

"Sometimes, bread is *all* I eat!"

"Well," says Noa, "long ago,
Egypt had a king, Pharaoh.
He made the Jewish people slaves.
Moses saved them. He was brave.

He begged Pharaoh, 'Let them go!'
Pharaoh told him, 'No, no, no.'
They escaped across the sand,
running to the holy land.

With no time for bread to rise,

it came out flat, about this size."

Kids all nod. The story's done. . . .

Noa looks at everyone.

Is there more that she could do?

Let them *taste* Passover too?

FOOD FOR THOUGHT

So the next day, she comes back
with something special in her pack.

When her friends all start to trade,
Noa says, "See what I've made!
'Cause I couldn't swap before,
this time, I just brought in more!"

"Mmm," her friends say as they munch.

"*Matzah* has a tasty crunch!"

Pat says, "This stuff's nice with cheese."

Pete says, "I'd like seconds, please!"

After seven Pesach days,
Noa's launched a **matzah craze**!

Chocolate matzah, matzah brei . . .
then a matzah pizza pie!

Noa says, "Now you can see
what my matzah means to me.

Sharing it with you this way
makes a perfect holiday!"

About Passover

Passover is a week-long holiday celebrated in the spring, when we remember the exodus of the Jews from slavery in Egypt. Passover starts with a seder, a festive meal of prayers, readings, songs, and the tasting of symbolic foods. No bread is eaten during Passover. Instead, we eat matzah.

About the Author

Jamie Kiffel-Alcheh regularly writes for *National Geographic KIDS*. Her many books include *Hard Hat Cat*, *Kol Hakavod: Way to Go!*, *A Hoopoe Says Oop!*, *Rah! Rah! Mujadara*, *Can You Hear a Coo, Coo?* and *Listen! Israel's All Around*. She is also a lyricist for pop songs, advertisements, and motion pictures. She lives in Burbank, California.

About the Illustrator

Lauren Gallegos has illustrated many children's books since she earned her Bachelors of Fine Arts in Illustration from Cal State Fullerton. She continues to improve her craft and illustrate for young children. She lives in the Washington, DC, area with her husband and young daughter.